# Secret PRINCESSES

# Gymnastics Glory

## ROSIE BANKS

Wishing Star Palace

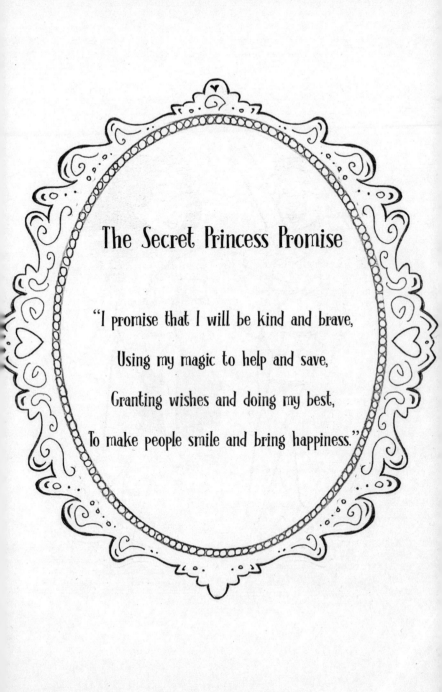

# The Secret Princess Promise

"I promise that I will be kind and brave,

Using my magic to help and save,

Granting wishes and doing my best,

To make people smile and bring happiness."

# CONTENTS

## CHAPTER ONE

# Trampoline Time

"Woo hoo!" cried Mia Thompson, bending her knees and leaping up in the air.

"Higher! Higher!" shrieked her little sister, Elsie.

Mia and Elsie were jumping on the new trampoline in their back garden. It had been a present for Elsie's birthday and the two girls loved bouncing on it together.

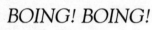

*BOING! BOING!*
Mia's long blonde
hair flew up in the
air as she bounced
up and down on the
trampoline's springy
surface.

"Yippee!" cried Mia
as she jumped up,
kicking her legs
out wide.

Elsie copied her
and then they both
flopped down on the
trampoline, giggling
and out of breath.

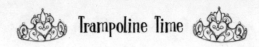 

"Can you do a flip?" Elsie asked Mia as they lay on their backs, trying to catch their breath.

Mia shook her head. "Too bad Charlotte doesn't live here any more," she said. "She'd know how to do all sorts of tricks."

Charlotte Williams was Mia's best friend, who had moved to California not long ago. Unlike Mia, who liked baking and doing crafts, Charlotte was very sporty. Even though the girls were total opposites, they had been the closest of friends ever since they were tiny.

Mia scrambled to her feet and pulled Elsie up too. "Come on," she told her sister. "Let's bounce again!"

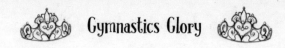 

Mia sprang up high enough to see over the fence into her neighbours' garden, with its neatly trimmed grass and tidy flower beds. Mia grinned. It was hard to believe that someone famous had once lived there!

The next-door neighbours had a daughter called Alice, who used to babysit Mia and Charlotte. But then Alice had won a TV talent competition and became a famous pop star. Now she travelled around the world giving concerts, but her parents still lived next door to Mia.

Thanks to Alice, Mia and Charlotte were still as close as ever even though they now lived very far apart. Because Alice wasn't just a pop star, she was also a Secret

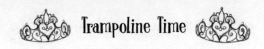 

Princess – someone who granted wishes using magic. Even more excitingly, she thought that Mia and Charlotte had the potential to be Secret Princesses too!

Alice had given the girls matching necklaces that allowed them to meet at an enchanted place called Wishing Star Palace. As part of their training, the girls

went on amazing adventures together,
helping people with magic.

As she bounced on the trampoline, Mia
wondered when she and Charlotte would
get to do magic together next.

"Help!" cried Elsie,
snapping Mia out of
her daydream.

Elsie was trying to do
a forward roll but she'd
got stuck. Her head
was on the trampoline
and her bottom was
in the air. She was
struggling to flip her
legs over her head.

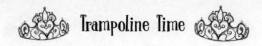 

Mia crouched down next to her sister. "There you go," she said, bringing Elsie's legs round.

Elsie sat up and sighed. "I'll never earn my gymnastics badge if I can't do a somersault," she said, pouting.

"You just need to keep practising," Mia reassured her. "You're nearly there."

As she helped Elsie practise forward rolls, Mia's thoughts drifted back to Wishing Star Palace. She and Charlotte were on the third stage of their training. So far, they had granted two wishes. If they granted two more, they would each earn a magic sapphire ring that flashed in warning when danger was nearby.

Pulling out the collar of her T-shirt to peek at her necklace, Mia gave a little gasp. It was glowing!

"What's wrong, Mia?" Elsie asked her.

"Nothing," Mia said quickly. She smiled at her sister. "I just realised it's nearly time for your gymnastics class," she said. "You'd better go inside and get changed."

Elsie climbed down from the trampoline and trotted across the garden. Once Elsie was indoors, Mia pulled out her necklace. It was a gold pendant shaped like half of a heart, hanging from a delicate chain. Two brilliant blue sapphires, which they earned for the two wishes they had granted, were embedded in the pendant.

Mia's tummy leaped
with excitement as
she clutched the
glowing half-heart.
"I wish I could see
Charlotte," she said.

Golden light flowed
out of the pendant and swirled around Mia.
The whirlpool of light lifted her off the
trampoline. Glancing down, Mia saw the
garden getting smaller and smaller beneath
her. She didn't worry about Elsie or her
mum missing her – time would magically
stand still here while she was away.

A moment later, Mia found herself in
another garden, high up in the clouds.

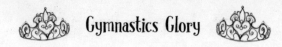
But this one had pink and pale blue candyfloss bushes and trees with candy apples growing on them! In the distance, Wishing Star Palace rose up majestically, its heart-shaped windows gleaming and purple flags flying from its four turrets. Mia's heart swelled with pride. She was so lucky to be here!

Looking down, Mia saw that her T-shirt and skirt had magically transformed into her silky gold princess dress. Her feet, which had been bare, were now wearing sparking ruby slippers.

"Yoo hoo, Mia!" cried a voice. "Over here!" A girl in a pale pink princess dress was waving at her from across the lawn.

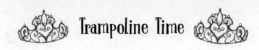
"Charlotte!" called Mia, running over to her friend.

Charlotte's brown curls bobbed in the air as as she sprinted across the grass to meet Mia. When they reached each other, the girls grabbed hands and spun around and around, beaming at each other.

"It's so good to see you," said Charlotte, when they had stopped spinning.

"I was just talking about you," Mia said. "Elsie got a new trampoline for her birthday and wanted to know how to do a back-flip."

"Like this!" said Charlotte, kicking off her ruby slippers. She ran across the grass and back-flipped in the air. She made it look so easy!

Mia clapped. "I knew you'd be able to do one."

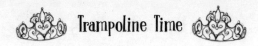 

 Charlotte smoothed
down her dress
and adjusted the
diamond tiara on her
head. It was exactly
the same as the one
Mia was wearing.
They'd earned them
for completing the
first stage of their
princess training.

"Should we go inside?" Mia asked.

Charlotte nodded and adjusted her
sparkling red shoes. As they got closer to
the palace they saw that there was a red
carpet lining the pathway to the front door.

Above the door, a glowing sign jutted out, like the sort above a cinema.

Charlotte stared at the sign, puzzled. "That wasn't there before."

"Welcome to the World Premiere of *Charming*," said Mia, reading the words on the sign aloud.

"Do you think that means we're going to watch a film?" said Charlotte.

"Maybe," said Mia, her blue eyes shining with excitement. "Let's go and find out!"

24

## CHAPTER TWO
# A Movie Star Princess

Holding hands, the girls ran down the red carpet and stepped inside the palace.

"Do you remember how to get to the Movie Room?" Charlotte asked Mia.

"I think it's upstairs," Mia replied. They'd only been in the Movie Room once before, when they'd had a sleepover at the palace. Wishing Star Palace was enormous, so it

was easy to get lost!

The girls climbed up a sweeping staircase. Pausing at the top, Mia thought for a moment. "I'm pretty sure it's this way," she said, pointing down a long corridor.

Mia and Charlotte headed down the hallway, which was lined with paintings of Secret Princesses.

"Look!" said Charlotte, stopping in front of a portrait of a princess with bright red hair holding a cake shaped like Wishing Star Palace. "Princess Sylvie's portrait is back!" The princess in the portrait winked at them.

On their last adventure, Mia and Charlotte had helped make a girl called

Ruby's wish of winning a baking contest
come true. But that wasn't all – they had
also freed Princess Sylvie from a curse
that had made her forget she was a Secret
Princess!

Mia frowned, glancing at two gaps on the
wall. "But Kiko and Sophie's portraits are
still under Princess Poison's spell."

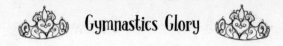 

Princess Poison used to be a Secret Princess until she went bad. Now she spoiled wishes instead of granting them, and kept the power for herself. Her latest plan was her most terrible. She'd tricked Princess Sophie, who was an artist, into displaying four paintings at an art gallery called the Hexagon. Princess Poison had cursed the portraits of Cara, Sylvie, Kiko and Sophie, making them forget that they were Secret Princesses. The four princesses didn't even believe in magic any more!

The only way to break the spell and get the portraits back was for the princesses to return to Wishing Star Palace. That was a lot trickier than it sounded, because they

didn't remember it existed!

"We broke the curse on Cara and Sylvie's portraits," Charlotte reminded Mia. "And we'll get the other two portraits back, too. But first we've got to find the princesses who are still here!"

Mia and Charlotte hurried down a hallway and found themselves outside a door with a gold sign that said "Movie Room". Inside, Secret Princesses in elegant evening gowns sat on huge, squashy velvet sofas. A princess whose strawberry-blonde hair had red streaks in it waved to them. Princess Alice!

"Sit next to me!" Alice called, patting a red sofa that matched her sequinned gown.

"The film is just about to start!"

As the lights dimmed, Mia and Charlotte snuggled up next to Alice. The film was about a brave heroine trying to protect her land from evil Queen Alexa, who had frizzy black hair and a long black cape. Mia loved the film, but she would have enjoyed it even

more if mean Queen Alexa hadn't reminded
her of Princess Poison. She couldn't stop
thinking about the spell on Kiko and
Sophie. It would be much more fun if they
were there, watching too. Instead they
didn't even remember that magic existed!

When the lights came up, everyone
clapped.

"Did you like the movie?" Alice asked
Charlotte and Mia.

"It was great," said Charlotte. "Was that
you singing on the soundtrack?"

Alice nodded happily. "Yes, I wrote the
theme song."

"Is that why the premiere was here at
Wishing Star Palace?" asked Mia.

"Not quite," said Alice, smiling. "Come on – there's someone I'd like you to meet."

The girls followed Alice to a cluster of princesses congratulating someone. When the group parted, Mia gasped. It was Queen Alexa!

Her frizzy dark hair was perfectly straight now, and she was wearing a pretty lemon yellow gown instead of a cape. But it was definitely her! Mia stepped back nervously.

"Don't look so frightened," Alice said, chuckling. "There's nothing to be afraid of," she went on, showing them her sapphire ring. The blue stone wasn't flashing, so there was no danger near. "This is Princess Grace. She's a Secret Princess, but in the real world she's an actress."

"Hello!" said Grace. Her warm smile was very different to Queen Alexa's nasty scowl. "You must be Mia and Charlotte. The others have told me so much about you I feel like we're friends already."

"You were really scary in the movie," Mia told her shyly.

"Thanks!" said Grace. "Can you guess who I based the character on?"

33

Mia remembered who Queen Alexa had reminded her of. "Princess Poison!" she exclaimed.

"That's right!" said Grace, grinning. "She's the nastiest person I've ever met, so that's how I played the evil queen."

"Have you been in any other movies?" Charlotte asked Grace.

"I've had small parts, but this film was my big break," said Grace. "The only bad thing was that I was so busy filming I haven't been able to visit Wishing Star Palace very much."

"We're really happy to have you back," said Alice, giving her friend a hug.

"Is it amazing being an actress?" Charlotte

asked Grace. Mia didn't like being on stage, but her best friend loved performing.

"Yes, but not as amazing as being a Secret Princess," said Grace.

"Who wants popcorn?" called Princess Sylvie, coming into the Movie Room holding a cake shaped like a box of popcorn.

"Um, that's a cake – not popcorn," Charlotte whispered in Mia's ear.

"You should do the honours, Grace,"

Sylvie said, handing her a knife.

"Yum!" said Grace. "I've missed your baking, Sylvie."

Grace cut into the cake and popcorn burst out of the centre. *POP! POP! POP!*

Clapping her hands in delight, Grace said, "That's so cool, Sylvie!"

"I should have known," said Charlotte, laughing. "Sylvie's cakes are NEVER ordinary."

Sylvie handed Mia and Charlotte each a massive slice of cake.

"This is delicious," said Mia, trying a bite.

"Mmm-hmm," mumbled Charlotte, her mouth full of cake.

"When I was under Princess Poison's spell I wouldn't have believed a cake like this was possible," said Sylvie. "How can I ever thank you girls for making me believe in magic again?"

"You could let us have second helpings," suggested Charlotte cheekily.

"I don't think we'll have time for that," said Mia. Sylvie's wand, and all of the other princesses' wands, had started glowing. "Some has a wish that needs to be granted!"

Charlotte quickly set down her plate of cake. "Can we go?" she begged Sylvie. "Please!"

"We really want to earn our third sapphire," Mia explained.

"That's fine with me," said Sylvie.

"If you see Princess Poison, tell her to go and see my movie," Grace said, winking.

"If we see Princess Poison, we'll tell her that we're going to break the curse on Kiko and Sophie," said Charlotte.

The Secret Princesses cheered and wished the girls good luck. Mia and Charlotte ran to the nearest of the palace's four towers. They pounded up a long, twisting staircase to a small room with an oval-shaped mirror.

"There she is," said Mia, staring at the image of a girl in the glass. Her light brown hair was scraped back in a high ponytail and she was stretching her arms high above her head. "That's who we need to help."

Writing magically appeared on the mirror and Charlotte read it aloud:

> "A wish needs granting, adventures await,
> Call Layla's name, don't hesitate!"

"Layla!" Mia and Charlotte exclaimed together.

The girl's image vanished and was replaced with swirling golden light. Mia's tummy fluttered with excitement.

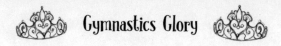 

As she and Charlotte touched the mirror, Mia felt herself being pulled into a tunnel of light. Where would the magic take them this time?

## CHAPTER THREE
# Layla's Wish

Mia landed gently on a soft, springy blue mat. Her gold princess dress had been transformed into a long-sleeved turquoise leotard with a shiny silver starburst on the chest.

"Cool leotard," said Charlotte, whose dress had changed into a purple velour leotard and tight black shorts.

"Too bad I can't even do a cartwheel,"
said Mia, grinning.

Looking around, Mia saw that they
were in a gymnasium. Brightly coloured

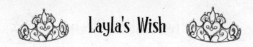 

banners saying "Regional Champions" hung down from the ceiling. Girls in leotards were practising on balance beams, uneven bars and vaults. Nobody had noticed Mia and Charlotte's sudden arrival, thanks to the magic, but the gymnasts were all concentrating so hard on their exercises that the girls probably could have parachuted in playing ukuleles and nobody would have paid any attention!

"Layla must be here somewhere," Charlotte said.

Mia scanned the room, trying to find the girl from the mirror.

"Wait – is that her?" Mia asked as she spotted a girl with a long brown ponytail.

Gymnastics Glory

The girl's white leotard became a blur as
she did a complicated sequence of tumbling
moves, twisting and flipping in the air.

"Wow!" said Charlotte, whistling. "She's
really good."

Layla
frowned and
rotated her left
ankle around in
circles.

"She doesn't
look very
happy though,"
said Mia.

"Let's go and talk to her," said Charlotte.
"Maybe we can find out what's wrong."

The girls went over to Layla, who was now rummaging in her kit bag.

"Phew!" Layla said, pulling something small out of one of the bag's pockets. Noticing the girls, she smiled and showed them a key ring shaped like a four-leafed clover. "For a second I thought I'd lost my lucky charm."

"I don't think you need luck," said Charlotte enthusiastically. "That tumbling was awesome."

"Thanks," said Layla. "But believe me – I do need luck. There are a lot of really talented gymnasts here today. Are you two trying out for a place on the Star Squad too?"

Charlotte shook her head. "No," she said. "We're just watching. I'm Charlotte, by the way, and this is Mia."

"My name's Layla," Layla told them, tightening her ponytail.

"What's the Star Squad?" Mia asked her.

"It's for advanced gymnasts. You get to compete with other squads at meets," explained Layla. "The Star Squad has won loads of competitions. Everyone wants to train here because the coach is amazing." She showed them a display cabinet full of trophies. "Some of the gymnasts she's coached have even won international medals. I really wish that I could get on the team!"

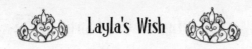

Catching Charlotte's eye, Mia winked
at her. So that was Layla's wish!

Layla took some stretchy tape out of
her bag and started wrapping it around
her ankle.

"What's wrong with your ankle?" Charlotte asked her.

"A few months ago I twisted it when I was practising my floor exercise," Layla said, winding the white tape tightly around and around her ankle. "I couldn't do gymnastics for weeks."

"Oh, no!" said Mia. "Is it better now?"

"My doctor says it's fine," Layla said. She'd finished taping her ankle and was flexing her foot up and down. "Floor exercise used to be my best event, but now I'm scared of doing my routine." Layla bit her lip anxiously.

"I can understand that you feel a bit nervous," Charlotte said sympathetically.

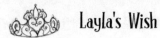
"But I'm sure you'll be fine."

A petite, dark-haired lady walked on to the floor mats and clapped her hands. Mia and Charlotte gasped in recognition. It was Princess Kiko!

"I'm Coach Kiko," she said, smiling at the gymnasts. "Try-outs for the Star Squad will begin shortly, but first can everyone please come and register."

"Gotta go," said Layla. She went over to Kiko, who was handing out paper numbers for the gymnasts to pin on their leotards.

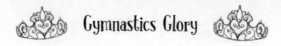 

"We need to talk to Kiko," Mia said. "Maybe we can convince her to go back to Wishing Star Palace and break Princess Poison's curse!"

Charlotte and Mia stood at the back of the queue. When they finally reached the front, Kiko smiled at them. "Your necklaces are so cute," she told the girls. "I love how they match."

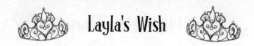 

"Thanks," said Charlotte. "They're magic – just like yours."

Kiko glanced down at her pendant, which was a leaping gymnast. "I don't know what you mean," she said, sounding confused.

"We're training to become Secret Princesses like you," Mia said.

"I'm afraid I can't train you to be princesses," Kiko said, shaking her head. "But I can train you to be excellent gymnasts." She gave them each a number to pin on their leotards.

"Oh no," said Mia, feeling terrified.

Charlotte smiled at the look on her friend's face. "We're not trying out. We're just here to support Layla."

"Oh, well, I'm sure she's glad to have you as cheerleaders," said Kiko, smiling.

Kiko gathered the gymnasts together and led a stretching session.

"Kiko didn't believe us, did she?" Mia asked Charlotte.

"No," replied Charlotte. "But she will. We'll get her to believe in magic again."

"And help Layla make the team," added Mia. She looked over at Layla, whose legs were stuck out straight in front of her, toes pointed. Bending forward from her waist, Layla rested her tummy flat on her thighs. "Wow – she's really flexible."

Charlotte nodded. "She's really good. I'm sure she'll make the team."

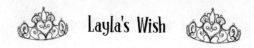 

At Kiko's command, the gymnasts bent forward, flexing their feet.

"Hey, what do gymnasts and bananas have in common?" Charlotte asked Mia.

"I don't know," said Mia. "But I'm pretty sure you're going to tell me."

"They can both do splits," said Charlotte, grinning.

Mia giggled but stopped laughing when a short, tubby man in a tight green warm-up suit marched into the gym. A dark-haired girl in a green leotard trailed behind him nervously, looking as if she'd rather be anywhere else.

"Oh no," groaned Mia, nudging Charlotte. "Here comes trouble."

"We're here for the try-outs," the man announced loudly. He was Hex, Princess Poison's assistant.

"You've missed most of the warm-up," said Kiko, as the gymnasts arched their backs into bridges. "You should stretch first."

"She'll be fine," Hex said, shoving the girl forward. Her name was Jinx and Princess Poison was training her to spoil wishes.

Charlotte turned to Mia, her hazel eyes wide with alarm. "You know what this means, don't you?"

Mia nodded grimly. Princess Poison wanted to spoil Layla's wish!

## CHAPTER FOUR
# A Sticky Situation

The girls eyed Jinx suspiciously as she fumbled with her paper number, trying to pin it on to her green leotard.

"Hurry up!" Hex snapped. He grabbed the number out of Jinx's hand and pinned it on to her.

"Ouch!" cried Jinx, as Hex jabbed her with a pin.

"We'll have to keep an eye on them," said Mia. "They're going to try and stop Layla from making the team."

When the gymnasts had finished their warm-up, the girls went over to Layla, who was squeezing her four-leafed clover keyring. "How are you feeling?" Mia asked her.

"A bit nervous," said Layla. She held up her good luck charm. "But I should be fine as long as I have this."

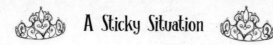 

"What's the first event?" Charlotte asked.

"Vault," replied Layla.

Mia and Charlotte sat down on a bench at the side of the gymnasium and watched the gymnasts do their vaults. A girl in a hot pink leotard ran down the padded runway, jumped on to a springboard and did a twisting flip over the vault. On her landing, she wobbled slightly and took a step backwards before raising her hands above her head.

Mia glanced at Charlotte questioningly. It looked amazing to her, but Charlotte knew much more about gymnastics.

"Not bad," murmured Charlotte. "But she'll get a deduction for the landing."

The gymnast returned to the runway, saluted Kiko and then vaulted again.

"Why does she get another go?" asked Mia.

"They each get to do two vaults," Charlotte explained. "Their score is an average of the two vaults."

As they watched the gymnasts vault, Mia realised that Layla was right – there were a lot of talented gymnasts trying out for a spot on Kiko's team!

"Number 15?" called Kiko.

"That's you!" hissed Hex, giving Jinx a push.

Jinx walked slowly to the end of the runway. Raising her arms above her head,

Jinx saluted Kiko as all the gymnasts had done. She ran down the runway, jumped on

to the springboard and … *SPLAT!*

Jinx bellyflopped on to the vault.

"Ouch!" said Charlotte, wincing. "That's got to hurt."

Shamefaced, Jinx scrambled over the vault and dropped down on the landing mat.

"That was rubbish!" Hex shrieked at her.

"Don't worry," said Kiko, as Jinx returned

to the runway with flaming cheeks. "You still have your second vault."

Jinx's next attempt was even worse. She jumped off the springboard and managed to awkwardly propel herself over the vault, but landed flat on her bottom!

"Oh dear," said Mia. Despite all the trouble Jinx had caused on their last two adventures, Mia couldn't help feeling a bit sorry for her.

Hex marched over to Jinx and handed her a bottle filled with a bright orange sports drink. He whispered something in her ear, waving his hands angrily.

"I don't know what they're up to," Charlotte said. "But Layla's in no danger

of losing a place on the team to Jinx – she's terrible."

Layla went over and put a consoling hand on Jinx's shoulder. "There are three more events to go," she told her. "I'm sure you'll do better in those."

Jinx nodded and unscrewed her bottle top. *FIZZ!* The orange drink spewed out and sprayed all over Layla's white leotard!

"Well, well. This is a sticky situation, isn't it?" said Hex, smirking at Mia and Charlotte.

"I'm so sorry," Jinx told Layla as Hex led her away.

"It's OK," Layla said, shaking drops of orange liquid off her hands. "It was an accident."

Mia glared at Princess Poison's helpers. "That was no accident," she muttered to Charlotte.

"Nope," Charlotte said. "I'm pretty sure Hex shook that bottle up before he gave it to Jinx."

"Number 20," called Kiko. "You're next."

"That's me," said Layla. She grabbed

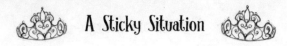 

a towel from her kit bag and frantically blotted her leotard. It did nothing to remove the big orange stain across her chest. "What am I going to do?" she wailed. "I'm all sticky and there's no time for me to get changed."

Mia knew exactly what they needed to do – it was time to make a wish! "We can help you," she told Layla. "Right, Charlotte?"

Charlotte nodded and they held their glowing pendants together, forming a perfect heart. "I wish for a new leotard for Layla," said Charlotte.

Light shot out of the heart and Layla's stained leotard was magically transformed. It was now bright red with a pattern of sparkling diamante stars.

"Oh my gosh!" said Layla, looking at her new leotard in astonishment. "It's absolutely gorgeous, but how did you do that?"

"Number 20!" Kiko called more loudly.

"We'll explain later," said Charlotte. "You need to go and do your vaults."

"Good luck!" called Mia.

Layla hurried over to the runway and saluted Kiko, arching her back and raising both arms in the air. With a look of determination on her face, she sprinted down the runway and did a powerful handspring on to the vault. Pushing off with her hands, she twisted in the air.

As Layla tucked her knees and prepared to land, there was a bright flash of light.

64

Distracted by the light, Layla's head jerked
up and she stumbled on her landing.

Mia turned around to see where the light
had come from and saw Hex standing on
the sidelines. He was taking pictures with a
camera with a bright white flash.

"Hex did that on purpose," Mia said angrily. "He knew the flash would distract Layla."

"I'm not going to let him spoil her second vault," Charlotte said.

Charlotte started storming over to Hex, but as she stepped on to the springy gym floor one of the assistant coaches stopped her. "Sorry – only gymnasts trying out for the team are allowed on the equipment right now."

Mia still had the two paper numbers Kiko had given them, when she thought they wanted to try out. "Here – put this on," she told Charlotte.

Charlotte quickly pinned on the number

and crossed the floor with a series of aerials,
round-offs and back-flips. She landed right
in front of Hex, taking him by surprise.
There was a brief struggle but Charlotte

snatched the
camera away
from him just
in time.
Layla was
at the end
of the
runway,
about to

begin her second vault. After presenting to
Kiko, she sprinted down the runway, lifting
her knees high and pumping her arms.

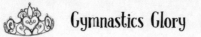 

Cartwheeling on to the springboard, she did a back handspring on to the vault then flipped in the air. She landed in a squatting position, her arms stuck out in front of her for balance. Straightening up, she saluted Kiko proudly.

"Layla was awesome," said Charlotte, trotting up to Mia with Hex's camera.

Mia beamed at her best friend. "So were you!"

## CHAPTER FIVE
# Danger in the Gym

Once all the gymnasts had completed their vaults, Kiko approached Mia and Charlotte. "That was brilliant tumbling," she told Charlotte. "Did you want to try out for the team after all?"

"No," Charlotte said, taking the paper number off her leotard. She pointed at Hex, who was sitting with Jinx, scowling.

"I just needed to get that man to stop taking photos. The flash on his camera was distracting the gymnasts."

"Thanks for doing that," Kiko said. "Are you sure you don't want to try out? You're really good."

"I'm positive," Charlotte said. "We're just here to grant someone's wish – just like you do. Remember?" She stared at Kiko, willing her to remember.

Kiko just shook her head in confusion. "Well, good luck with that," she said, sounding amused.

Kiko's sapphire ring caught Mia's eye. Blue light was flashing from the jewel. "Oh no!" Mia gasped. "Your magic ring is

70

flashing – there's danger nearby."

Kiko glanced down at her ring and smiled. "It's just light glinting off the gem," she said. "My ring isn't magic and the gym is perfectly safe as long as gymnasts remember to use the equipment properly. There's no danger here."

"Oh yes, there is,"
Charlotte muttered
under her breath as the
door opened and a tall,
woman wearing a tight
green tracksuit and
trainers walked into
the gym.

"Oh, great," groaned Mia as Princess
Poison tossed her streaked hair over her
shoulder and went to join Hex and Jinx.

Kiko went to the middle of the gym floor
and clapped her hands. "OK, gymnasts," she
called. "Nice work on your vaults. The next
event will be the uneven bars."

While the gymnasts prepared for their

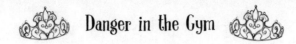 

uneven bar routines, Layla ran over to Mia and Charlotte, her ponytail bobbing.

"Great vault," Charlotte said.

"Thanks, but never mind about that," said Layla, waving away Charlotte's compliment. "I'm dying to know how you changed my leotard."

Mia and Charlotte exchanged looks. Would Layla believe them?

"We used magic," said Mia. She held up her pendant. "Our necklaces let us to make three wishes to help you."

"We're training to become Secret Princesses," said Charlotte. "And we're here to grant your wish of making the gymnastics team."

"Hang on a minute," said Layla. "You two can do MAGIC?"

"I know it's hard to believe," said Mia.

"No, I believe you," said Layla. "I

thought it must have been magic when my leotard changed like that and nobody else noticed. But why are you helping me? Everybody here is desperate to become part of the team."

"Yes, but you actually made a wish," said Mia, with a smile.

"And granting wishes is what Secret

Princesses do," said Charlotte, smiling. "We can't make you part of the team — that wouldn't be fair on everyone else, but we can help in other ways."

"That's so cool," said Layla happily. "I guess my key ring is bringing me good luck after all."

Mia and Charlotte sat with Layla as the gymnasts took turns on the uneven bars. A gymnast in a navy blue leotard dipped her hands in a basin full of white powder and rubbed it on her palms.

"What's she doing?" Mia asked Charlotte.

"It's chalk to stop her palms from getting slippery," Charlotte explained.

The gymnast gripped the lower bar and

swung around it twice, building up power. Letting go of the bottom bar, she swung to the higher bar. She raised her body into a handstand, her legs perfectly straight and her toes pointed.

"She must be really strong," said Mia, impressed.

Layla flexed the muscles in her arms. "We might not look it, but gymnasts are some of the strongest athletes around."

The gymnast in the blue leotard finished her routine, landing perfectly.

"She didn't make any mistakes," commented Mia.

"Yes, but it isn't just about not making mistakes," Charlott explained patiently.

"Kiko will also be considering how difficult the moves are."

"It all looks hard to me!" said Mia, laughing.

When it was Jinx's turn, Hex went over to the uneven bars with her. He produced a spray bottle and started squirting the bars.

"They're cheating!" cried Mia, standing up in outrage. "He's spraying something on the equipment!"

"Don't worry," Layla said. "He's just spraying water. It helps you grip the wooden bars. It isn't against the rules – I do it too."

Charlotte nodded her head, confirming what Layla had said. Mia sat down again, her face flushing red. It was normally

Charlotte who was loud, but Mia hated it when things were unfair! She couldn't shake the feeling that Hex was up to something sneaky – especially when he turned to them and smirked.

Cringing, Jinx went on her tiptoes and tried to pull herself up on to the top bar.

"Get on with it!" shouted Princess Poison.

"Do you need a boost?" Kiko asked her gently.

Jinx nodded gratefully. Grunting loudly, Hex lifted Jinx up, staggering as she groped for the wooden bar. Jinx dangled from the top bar, her legs flailing wildly.

"Don't just hang there!" shrieked Princess Poison. "Do something!"

Jinx kicked her legs out and struggled to hoist herself over the bar, her face turning red with effort.

"I can't bear to watch this," said Charlotte, covering her eyes.

Giving up, Jinx let go of the bars and flopped on to the mat.

Layla ran over and squatted down next to Jinx. "Are you all right?" she asked, her voice full of concern.

"I'm so bad," Jinx muttered.

"You just need more practice," said Layla encouragingly. She put her arm around Jinx's shoulder and helped her up. "Gymnastics isn't just about talent. It also takes a lot of hard work."

"That's right," said Kiko, overhearing her. "Making my team is the easy part – I expect my gymnasts to train very hard."

"That was terrible," Hex told Jinx, rudely pulling her away from Layla. He thrust the squirty bottle into Layla's hands. "You're next."

Layla squirted water on to the wooden bars. When she was finished, she raised her arm, signalling to Kiko that she was ready to begin her routine.

Somersaulting off a springboard, Layla grabbed the bottom bar. She swung around the bar, her legs straddled wide. Building up momentum, she flew across to the top bar but one of her hands slipped. She clung on with one hand, looking worried.

"Something's wrong," said Charlotte.

"Oh dear," said Hex, sneaking up behind them. "Layla's place on the team is *slipping* right out of her hands." He waved a squirty

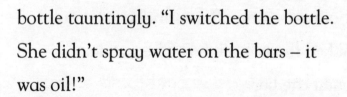

bottle tauntingly. "I switched the bottle. She didn't spray water on the bars – it was oil!"

Layla released the top bar, doing a difficult twist in the air. When she reached out to grasp the bottom bar, her hands slipped and she crashed on to the mat.

"Oh no!" Mia gasped.

"Keep going, Layla!" Charlotte shouted. Turning to Mia, she said, "We need to sort this out fast – Layla only has thirty seconds to get back on the bars or she'll be disqualified!"

The girls touched their pendants together and Mia said, "I wish the bars weren't slippery."

There was a flash of magical light. A moment later, Layla was back on her feet, pulling herself back up on the uneven bars. The rest of her routine was flawless as she swung effortlessly from bar to bar, twisting and turning in the air and dismounting without a wobble.

"You did really well to carry on after falling," Charlotte told her.

"I don't know what happened," Layla said, shaking her head. "I couldn't seem to grip the bars at first."

"It's because of them," said Mia, gesturing to where Jinx was with Hex and Princess Poison. "They tricked you into spraying oil on the bars, but we used a wish to fix it."

"Thank you so much for helping," said Jinx. "I just hope my fall didn't cost me a place on the Star Squad team."

"You did really difficult moves," said Charlotte. "And there are still two more events to go."

Just then, Kiko called out, "We're moving on to the balance beam now!"

Mia squeezed Layla's hand. "You'll be great – I know you will."

*As long as we can stop Princess Poison from causing more trouble,* she added silently.

## CHAPTER SIX
# A Difficult Balance

While Layla stretched, Mia and Charlotte watched the gymnasts perform on the balance beam. The gymnast in the hot pink leotard mounted the beam and dropped down into a back bend. She kicked her legs over her head, then pivoted on the narrow beam. Balancing on one leg, she gracefully lifted the other leg above her head.

"Whoa!" said Mia. "That beam is so narrow."

Layla nodded. "It's only four inches wide."

For her finale, the gymnast did three cartwheels along the beam, before somersaulting gracefully down on to the landing mat.

"She's definitely going make the team," Layla said, her voice wistful.

"I'm sure you will too," said Charlotte.

When it was Jinx's turn, she climbed up on to the beam and started walking along it, wobbling wildly.

"Why do they look so smug?" Mia said, staring at Princess Princess and Hex.

Princess Poison pointed her wand at Jinx.

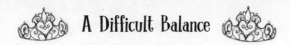 

A flash of magical green light hit Jinx and
she suddenly did a beautiful arabesque.
Then she leaped along the balance beam,
her legs scissoring high up in the air.

"Wow!" said Layla. "Those are advanced
moves. I guess she was just nervous earlier."

Kiko looked astonished at Jinx's amazing transformation too. She kept glancing down at her clipboard, as if checking whether Jinx was the same gymnast who couldn't get over the vault and had fallen off the bars earlier.

"She's only doing well because Princess Poison did a spell to help her," Charlotte told Layla crossly. "They're cheating."

"We won't let them get away with it," Mia promised Layla.

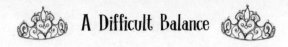
When it was Layla's turn, she rubbed chalk on her hands and feet. Then, planting her hands firmly on the balance beam, she raised her body into a handstand. Dropping her legs down, she skipped along the beam, kicking her legs high in the air. Pivoting with perfect poise, she sank down on one knee and did three forward rolls across the beam.

Mia and Charlotte marched over to where Princess Poison and Hex were congratulating Jinx.

"Yes, well done," said Charlotte. "You deserve a medal FOR CHEATING."

"Layla doesn't need to cheat," said Mia. "She's really talented."

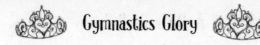
"Aw … Are you feeling sad that I helped Jinx with my magic?" Princess Poison asked them. "Don't worry, I have enough magic for your little friend, too."

She pointed her wand at Layla and spat out a spell:

"Make that beam grow even thinner,
Then we'll see who is the winner!"

There was a flash of green light. Horrified, Mia and Charlotte watched as the balance beam shrank, becoming even narrower.

Layla did a tuck jump, bringing her knees up high and turning around in the air. But when she landed, her arms windmilled wildly as she tried to keep her balance. She was going to fall!

"We have to help her!" Mia said. "We need to use our last wish!"

Charlotte pushed her pendant next to Mia's. They were glowing very faintly now, because there was only a little magic left.

"I wish for the balance beam to go back to its normal size," Charlotte said quickly.

With a flash of light, the balance beam was restored to its usual width. Looking

relieved, Layla performed the rest of her routine beautifully. She pirouetted on the beam and did a handspring, before finishing with a difficult round-off dismount.

Layla hurried over to the girls. "I must have been really nervous. The beam felt even narrower than usual today."

"It *was* narrower than usual," Charlotte said. "Because Princess Poison put a spell on it."

"That's so unfair," said Layla, shocked.

"I know," said Mia. "But it didn't stop you from doing a great routine."

Layla sighed. "The next event is the floor exercise. That's how I hurt my ankle." She looked down at her strapped ankle nervously.

"Try to stay positive," said Charlotte. "Maybe you should do some ankle stretches while you're waiting."

"Good idea," said Layla.

Once Layla had gone off to stretch, Princess Poison sidled up to Mia and

Charlotte. "There's one more event to go," said Princess Poison, her cold green eyes focussed on their necklaces. "What a pity you don't have any more wishes left."

"We don't need any more wishes," Charlotte told her. "Layla is a really talented gymnast."

"We'll see about that," said Princess Poison, sauntering off.

A lively tune started playing and the gymnast in the navy blue leotard began performing an energetic floor exercise. She leaped and tumbled across the floor, her movements in time to the music. The other gymnasts clapped their hands to the beat, urging her on.

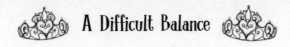
"This is so fun to watch," said Mia.

"It's even more fun to do," said Charlotte. "It mixes dance and gymnastics – two of my favourite things!"

"I bet you wish you could try out for Kiko's team," said Mia.

Charlotte shook her head. "I have a great gymnastics team back at home. Besides, nothing is more fun than granting someone's wish!"

When it was Jinx's turn to perform, she stood on the springy gym floor holding a long satin ribbon on a stick. Classical music boomed out of the speakers and she skipped across the floor, but got tangled up in the ribbon and tripped.

"What on earth is she doing?" said Charlotte. "You don't use ribbons in artistic gymnastics – only in rhythmic gymnastics."

Kiko, and all the other gymnasts, looked puzzled too.

Princess Poison pointed her wand and a flash of green light hit Jinx. Twirling the ribbon in the air, Jinx leaped across the gym floor. As the ribbon spiralled around her body, Jinx spun on her toes like a ballerina. She pranced and danced across the floor, the ribbon swirling around her. To finish, Jinx rolled on the ground and struck a dramatic pose.

"That was … interesting," said Mia.

"Yeah," said Charlotte. "Princess Poison

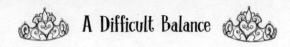 

obviously doesn't realise that rhythmic gymnastics is a completely different sport. I guess magic can't help her cheat at everything!"

They went over to Layla, who was rooting around frantically in her kit bag. "Where is it?" she wailed.

"What are you looking for?" Mia asked.

"My lucky key ring!" said Layla, her lip wobbling as she fought back tears. "I can't find it anywhere. I'm scared to do my floor routine without it."

"We'll help you look," said Charlotte. She and Mia started searching for the key ring.

"Looking for something?" Princess Poison said, dangling the key ring in front of them.

"You found it!" gasped Layla, reaching for her lucky charm.

"Not so fast!" said Princess Poison, snatching it away. She pointed her wand at the key ring and – *POOF!* – it vanished in a flash of green light.

"Looks like you're all out of luck!" cackled Princess Poison.

## CHAPTER SEVEN

# Hard Luck, Princess Poison

"I can't do it!" cried Layla, panicking. "I can't do my floor exercise without my lucky charm!"

"Yes, you can," said Charlotte. "You don't need luck because you've got talent."

"But what if I fall again?" said Layla.

"You're just being superstitious," said Mia.

"You can't let fear stop you from doing something you're really good at," Charlotte told her.

Layla let out a deep breath. "OK," she said. "I'll do it."

"You'll be amazing," said Mia, giving her a thumbs up.

Layla stepped on to the springy floor and raised her arms above her head, presenting to Kiko. As a jazzy show tune started playing, Layla launched into a lively routine. Smiling bravely, she bounced

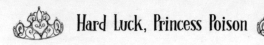 

and twirled to the upbeat music.

As they watched Layla's floor exercise, Princess Poison edged over to them. "I didn't think you'd want your little friend to get hurt again," she said.

"A silly key ring isn't going to prevent her from getting hurt," said Charlotte dismissively.

"Layla's making her own luck," said Mia.

"Yes," drawled Princess Poison. "She's got a real spring in her step. I really must do something about that." Narrowing her green eyes, she started muttering a spell.

**"It's time to give Layla a nasty shock.**
**Make the gym mats as hard as a rock."**

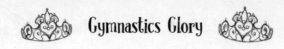
"Oh no," said Charlotte, clutching Mia. "If the mats turn hard, Layla could injure herself when she lands!"

"We need to stop her!" Mia gasped as Princess Poison slowly raised her wand and aimed it at the gym floor.

Charlotte leaped up and grabbed the long satin ribbon Jinx had used in her floor exercise. As green light poured out of the wand, Charlotte swirled the ribbon around her head like a lasso and whipped the wand out of Princess Poison's hand. The wand tumbled over and over before hitting the floor. Green light burst out of it – but instead of hitting the mats, it hit

Princess Poison instead!

The girls gasped. But before they could move, the music swelled and people started clapping along. Layla was nearing the end of her floor exercise. As they watched, she launched into a tricky tumbling pass, doing a double twist in the air.

Mia held her breath. Would Layla be able to make the landing?

Layla hit the mat – her knees bent,

her arms outstretched, and a look of
pure concentration on her face. Then,
straightening up, she beamed and saluted
at Kiko.

"She did it!" cried
Charlotte, giving
Mia a high five.
"That was a perfect
landing!"

As if on cue,
Princess Poison fell
on to the mat.
Her rigid body hit
the springy floor
with a bounce.
"Heeeeex, help

me!" she said, barely moving her lips. "I can't move!"

"Mistress!" cried Hex, running to her aid. "What's wrong?"

"It's her own fault," said Charlotte. "Her own magic turned her as hard as a rock."

Jinx bit her lip, as if she was trying hard not to laugh.

"Get me out of here!" Princess Poison said in a muffled voice, glaring at Mia and Charlotte. Hex hoisted up Princess Poison's shoulders, while Jinx lifted up her legs. Then together they carried her, stiff as a plank, out of the gym.

"Don't be too *hard* on yourself, Princess Poison," Charlotte called after them.

105

Mia giggled and swatted her friend affectionately.

"What?" said Charlotte, grinning. "She deserved that."

Layla bounded over to the girls. "How did I do?" she asked them.

"You were awesome!" said Charlotte.

"Do you think it was good enough to make the team?" Layla asked.

"Gather round, gymnasts!" called Kiko. "I've reached my decision."

"You won't have to wait long to find out!" said Mia.

The gymnasts sat in a circle on the floor. Several girls were holding hands anxiously as they waiting for Coach Kiko's verdict.

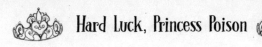 

Mia and Charlotte sat on either side of Layla, their arms around her shoulders.

"You all worked so hard today," said Kiko. "But unfortunately there are only three places open on my team."

"Please pick me, please pick me," Layla whispered to herself.

"Everyone's done really well, and gymnasts who haven't made the team should keep practising," said Kiko. "But without further ado, the three new members of Star Squad are ... Shanti Desai ..."

The girl in the hot pink leotard gasped.

"Isabel Cunningham ..."

The gymnast wearing navy blue squealed.

"And last, but not least, Layla Diaz!"

As the other gymnasts applauded, Mia and Charlotte hugged Layla.

Layla sat shaking her head as the other gymnasts headed into the locker room. "I can't believe I made the team," she said.

"I can," said Mia, smiling. "You're a

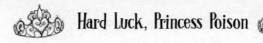

fantastic gymnast."

"Congratulations," said Kiko, shaking Layla's hand. "And welcome to the team!"

"Thanks so much," Layla said. "I didn't have much hope after I messed up my first vault and fell off the uneven bars."

"I wasn't looking for perfection," said Kiko, smiling. "I was looking for potential and the right attitude. Your routines had some seriously difficult moves in them, which told me you aren't afraid to challenge yourself. You also didn't let your mistakes throw you, which showed me that you never give up."

"There were so many other good gymnasts trying out today," Layla said.

Kiko nodded. "Yes, and you were very supportive of the other gymnasts, encouraging those less experienced than you. A team player like you will be a real asset to my squad."

Layla beamed with pride at Kiko's words, then she ran off to the locker room to get changed.

"I wish there was a trophy for the biggest smile," joked Kiko. "She'd definitely win!"

As soon as the words were out of her mouth, Kiko's necklace started glowing. Princess Sylvie appeared in front of them and presented Kiko with a gold trophy. The engraving on the bottom read *Biggest Smile*.

"What in the world …" said Kiko, staring at Sylvie. Her words trailed off as the gymnast on top of the trophy magically came to life. The gold figure tumbled in the air, doing cartwheels and back-flips in a blaze of glittering light.

"Can someone please tell me what's going on?" Kiko said.

"You wished for a trophy," said Mia.

"And the wish was granted because you're a Secret Princess."

"So is she," said Charlotte, going over to give Princess Sylvie a hug. "You can both do magic, even though you've forgotten."

"It's all true," Sylvie said, nodding. "The nasty woman in green put a curse on you so you don't remember."

"I did think there was something odd about her and the girl in the green leotard," said Kiko slowly.

"If you come to Wishing Star Palace with me, the spell will be broken," Sylvie said. "Then everything will make sense."

"Will you go with her?" Mia asked Kiko.

"Please?" begged Charlotte.

**Hard Luck, Princess Poison**

"Yes," said Kiko. "I will. Seeing is believing. Now I know that magic is real."

"Wonderful," said Sylvie. She smiled at the girls. "Thanks so much for granting Layla's wish." She touched her wand to their pendants and a sparkling new sapphire appeared in each one. "Shall I send you home now?" she asked them.

"Can we quickly say goodbye to Layla?" Charlotte asked.

"Of course," said Sylvie.

The girls ran into the locker room and found Layla packing up her bag.

"We've got to go," said Mia.

"Thanks so much for helping me," Layla said, hugging them.

"Good luck on the team," said Charlotte.

"You taught me I don't need luck," said Layla, grinning. "Just hard work and a positive attitude."

As they hurried back to the princesses, Mia said, "Just one more wish and then we'll earn our sapphire rings."

Charlotte grinned at her. "Hopefully we

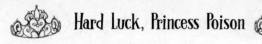

won't have to wait long."

"Ready to go?" Sylvie asked the girls.

They nodded. Sylvie waved her wand and light swirled around the girls.

"See you both at Wishing Star Palace soon," Mia called, waving to Kiko and Sylvie as the magic swept her away from the gym.

*BOING!* She landed with a gentle bounce on the trampoline in her back garden. Her leotard had changed back into the skirt and T-shirt she had been wearing before.

"Mia!" cried Elsie, charging out of the house into the back garden. "Watch!" Mia's little sister climbed on to the trampoline and did a perfect forward roll.

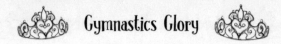

"Yay!" cheered Mia, clapping her hands.
"You did it!"

"Maybe I'll earn a badge at gymnastics
today," said Elsie.

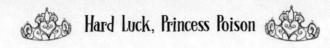 

"I'm sure you will!" said Mia. She glanced down at the three blue jewels twinkling on her pendant. Glowing with pride, she also felt sure that she and Charlotte would earn their sapphire rings very soon!

# The End

# Join Charlotte and Mia in their next Secret Princesses adventure

# Read on for a sneak peek!

# Picture Perfect

"Can you tie this please, Dad?" asked Charlotte Williams, handing her father the blue balloon she'd just blown up. As her dad tied a knot, Charlotte puffed into a yellow balloon. Blue and yellow were her little brothers' favourite colours.

"I think that's plenty," Charlotte's dad said, sticking balloons around the arched doorway that led from the hallway into the kitchen. Next, they stretched a banner reading Happy Birthday across the hall.

"The twins are going to be so surprised,"

Charlotte said, gazing at the decorations with satisfaction.

"I hope so!" said Dad, ruffling her brown curls.

Harvey and Liam had had their birthday party the previous weekend. They had gone go-karting, then shared a giant pizza with all their friends. But today was their actual birthday. Charlotte's mum had taken the twins to the beach, so that Charlotte and her dad could decorate the house and surprise the boys.

"It's still so weird that it's warm enough to go to the beach on their birthday," Charlotte said.

When their family had lived in England,

the twins' birthday party was always indoors
because it was too cold to play outside.
Since moving to sunny California, however,
they could go to the beach all year round!


Read Picture Perfect
to find out what
happens next!

# Layla's Favourite Famous Gymnasts

## Simone Biles
- Simone is the most decorated American gymnast, with 19 medals!
- Her signature move is a double-flip with a half-twist.
- She said she likes "a lot of sparkles" on her leotards.

## Laurie Hernandez
- Laurie is the youngest member of the all-girls Final Five gymnastics team.
- She is known for her dance moves and expressive face, which is why her nickname is "The Human Emoji"!
- If she wasn't a gymnast, Laurie has said she would want to be an actress.

## Gabby Douglas
- Gabby is the first ever American to win a gold medal in gymnastics both as an individual and in a team.
- She has her own Barbie doll that looks exactly like her.
- Her nickname is "The Flying Squirrel"!

## Aly Raisman
- Aly is the Captain and the oldest member of The Final Five, which is why her nickname is "Grandma"!
- She wants to design her own gymnastics clothes when she's older.
- Even though she has 11 gold medals, Aly describes herself as clumsy!

## Nadia Comăneci

- Nadia was the first gymnast in Olympic history to be awarded a perfect score of 10.
- After retiring from the sport, she helped to coach other female gymnasts.
- She now travels the world encouraging young girls to do gymnastics.

## Olga Korbut

- Olga was called "The Sparrow" because she was so small and could fly from one beam to the other!
- The "Korbut Flip" was named after her, which was a backwards flip from the high beam.

## Svetlana Khorkina
- She has eight gymnastics moves named after her!
- Her favourite piece of equipment were the bars, on which she performed elegant routines and was described as looking like a cat.
- She often would make up her own routines to perform, meaning that every one was different.

## Věra Čáslavská
- Before becoming a gymnast, Věra originally wanted to be a figure skater.
- She used to train in the forests near her home, using potato sacks as weights and logs as beams!
- Věra received a massive 22 medals during her career!

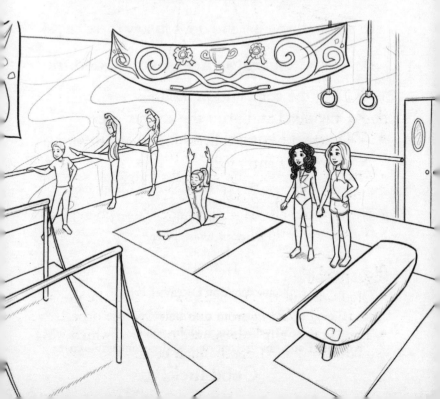

# ♥ WIN A PRINCESS GOODY BAG ♥

## Secret PRINCESSES

*What would you wish for?*

Design your own dress and win a Secret Princesses goody bag for you and your best friend!

Charlotte and Mia get to wear beautiful dresses at Wishing Star Palace, but now they want you to design one for them.

To enter all you have to do is follow these steps:

Go to **www.secretprincessesbooks.co.uk**

♥ Click the competition module
♥ Download and print the activity sheet
♥ Design a beautiful dress for Charlotte or Mia
♥ Send your entry to:

Secret Princesses: The Sapphire Collection Competition
Hachette Children's Group
Carmelite House
50 Victoria Embankment
London
EC4Y 0DZ

Closing date: 2nd December 2017

For full terms and conditions,
www.hachettechildrens.co.uk/
TermsandConditions/secretprincessesdresscompetition.page

## Good luck!

What would you wish for?

Lots of fun activities

Monthly treasure hunt

Create a secret profile

Earn princess points

Join in the fun at secretprincessesbooks.com

# Secret PRINCESSES

*What would you wish for?*

Are you a Secret Princess?

Join the Secret Princesses Club at:

## secretprincessesbooks.co.uk

Explore the magic of the
Secret Princesses and discover:

💜 Special competitions! 💜
💜 Exclusive content! 💜
💜 All the latest princess news! 💜

Open to UK and Republic of Ireland residents only
Please ask your parent/guardian for their permission to join

For full terms and conditions go to
secretprincessesbooks.co.uk/terms

## Sapphire13

Enter the special code above on the website to receive

# 50 Princess Points